**Dear Parents and Teachers,**

In an easy-reader format, **My Readers** introduce classic stories to children who are learning to read. Although favorite characters and time-tested tales are the basis for **My Readers**, the books tell completely new stories and are freshly and beautifully illustrated.

My Readers are available in three levels:

1 **Level One** is for the emergent reader and features repetitive language and word clues in the illustrations.

2 **Level Two** is for more advanced readers who still need support saying and understanding some words. Stories are longer with word clues in the illustrations.

3 **Level Three** is for independent, fluent readers who enjoy working out occasional unfamiliar words. The stories are longer and divided into chapters.

Encourage children to select books based on interests, not reading levels. Read aloud with children, showing them how to use the illustrations for clues. With adult guidance and rereading, children will eventually read the desired book on their own.

Here are some ways you might want to use this book with children:

- Talk about the title and the cover illustrations. Encourage the child to use these to predict what the story is about.
- Discuss the interior illustrations and try to piece together a story based on the pictures. Does the child want to change or adjust his first prediction?
- After children reread a story, suggest they retell or act out a favorite part.

My Readers will not only help children become readers, they will serve as an introduction to some of the finest classic children's books available today.

—LAURA ROBB
Educator and Reading Consultant

For activities and reading tips, visit myreadersonline.com

For Zoe—star of litter box, in-basket, and my heart
—T. F.

To Tonya
—O. I. & A. I.

SQUARE FISH

An Imprint of Macmillan Children's Publishing Group

Library of Congress Cataloging-in-Publication Data Available

ISBN 978-0-312-68168-5 (hardcover)
1 3 5 7 9 10 8 6 4 2

ISBN 978-0-312-68169-2 (paperback)
1 3 5 7 9 10 8 6 4 2

Book design by Patrick Collins/Véronique Lefèvre Sweet

Square Fish logo designed by Filomena Tuosto

First Edition: 2011

myreadersonline.com
mackids.com

This is a Level 2 book

LEXILE 280L

Harry Cat and Tucker Mouse
STARRING HARRY

Story by Thea Feldman

Illustrated by Olga and Aleksey Ivanov

Inspired by the characters from
The Cricket in Times Square
written by George Selden and illustrated by Garth Williams

SQUARE
FISH

Macmillan Children's Publishing Group
New York

Harry Cat and Tucker Mouse
were best friends.
They lived in a cozy drainpipe
in the Times Square subway station.

Every day, Harry and Tucker

had breakfast together.

Then they took a walk

and watched the crowds.

6

Every night, Tucker liked to stay home.

Harry always went out.

He loved the theater.

One night, Harry

saw a brand-new play.

People onstage

talked and talked.

Harry was bored.

He looked at the crowd.

They seemed bored too.

Just then, someone
walked onto the stage.
She was carrying a big fish.
Harry didn't stop to think.
He jumped!

Harry grabbed the fish
and ran off the stage.

11

The crowd began to laugh.

And clap.

And stand and cheer.

"Can you do this every night?"

asked the man in charge.

Harry purred.

He was saying yes.

Harry ran home to tell Tucker.

"Harry, that's wonderful!"

said Tucker, yawning.

"Let's talk about it

in the morning."

But Harry slept late

the next morning.

He was tired from his new job.

So Tucker had breakfast alone.

When Harry finally woke up,
he said, "I'm glad you ate.
You shouldn't wait to have
breakfast with me anymore.
I may be tired a lot now."

Harry *was* tired a lot.

He slept later and later every day.

Tucker was alone
more and more every day.

He took walks by himself.

He watched the crowds by himself.

It wasn't much fun without Harry.

One day, Tucker

couldn't stand it any longer.

He shouted,

"Harry, I never see you anymore!"

"I know," Harry said.

"I miss you too.

Please come to the theater tonight.

At least you can see me onstage!"

"That's not what I mean,"
said Tucker.

"You know I like to stay home
at night."

Harry looked sad.

"Oh, all right," said Tucker.

"I'll come."

"Thank you," said Harry.

That night, Tucker went
to Harry's play.
Tucker saw that Harry was
the best part of the whole show.
After the play, Tucker watched
everyone crowd around Harry.

They praised him
and patted his head.
Tucker couldn't get
anywhere near him.

25

Tucker walked home alone.

He was happy for Harry,

but he was sad for himself.

"Harry is a star now,"

he said. "I have to let him go."

Tucker tried not to cry.

When Tucker got home,

Harry was already there!

"Why so sad?"

Harry asked.

"Harry!" cried Tucker.

"Why are you here?

I thought you wanted to be

with your fans."

29

"I'd rather be with you,"
said Harry.

"Really?" asked Tucker.

"Really," said Harry.

"I quit the play tonight."

"Why?" asked Tucker.

"They can find another cat.
I missed my best friend,"
said Harry.

"Me?" asked Tucker.

"You," said Harry.

Then Harry yawned.

"Let's talk about it more

in the morning," he said.

Tucker yawned too.

"Harry," he said,

"you'll always be a star to me."